A Giant First-Start Reader

This easy reader contains only 40 different words, repeated often to help the young reader develop word recognition and interest in reading.

Basic word list for *Easter Parade*

a	eggs	more
and	everyone	Nancy
are	for	no
at	goes	now
baskets	has	paints
boom	help	parade
box	helps	she
Bunny	here	the
but	hop	there
candy	in	what
chirp	is	when
comes	look	who
Easter	makes	will
		with

Easter Parade

Written by Eileen Curran

Illustrated by Joan E. Goodman

Troll Associates

Library of Congress Cataloging in Publication Data

Curran, Eileen.
   Easter parade.

    Summary: With Nancy's help, the Easter Bunny has
something to make everyone's Easter happy, until it
suddenly becomes clear that there is nothing left for
little Nancy.
    1. Children's stories, American. [1. Easter—Fiction.
2. Animals—Fiction] I. Goodman, Joan E., ill.
II. Title.
PZ7.C9298Eas   1985   [E]   84-8630
ISBN 0-8167-0353-1 (lib. bdg.)

Chirp! Chirp! Here is Nancy.

Nancy helps the Easter Bunny.

She helps with the Easter parade.

Nancy paints the eggs.

She makes the baskets.

She makes the candy.

When Easter comes, hop, hop,
hop goes the Easter Bunny.

And chirp, chirp, chirp goes Nancy!

Now everyone has Easter eggs.

And everyone has Easter baskets.

And everyone has Easter candy.

Everyone but Nancy!

There are no more Easter eggs.

There are no more Easter baskets.

There is no more Easter candy.

Now who will help Nancy?

Hop! Hop! Hop!

There goes the Easter Bunny.

Boom! Boom! Boom!

There goes the Easter parade.

Chirp! Chirp!
Here comes Nancy.

The Easter Bunny has a box for Nancy.
What is in the box?

Look at Nancy.

Boom! Boom! Boom!

What a parade!

Chirp! Chirp! Here is Nancy.